this
strawberry book
belongs to

for
Mila

STRAWBERRY MOTHER GOOSE

Copyright © 1975 by One Strawberry, Inc.
All rights reserved
Printed in the United States of America
Library of Congress Catalog Card Number: 75-3808
ISBN: Trade 0-88470-016-X, Library 0-88470-017-8
strawberry books • distributed by Larousse & Co., Inc.
572 Fifth Avenue, New York, N.Y. 10036
Weekly Reader Books Edition

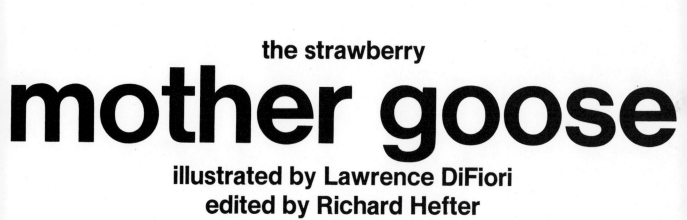

the strawberry
mother goose

illustrated by Lawrence DiFiori
edited by Richard Hefter

a strawberry book®

Pease porridge hot,
Pease porridge cold,
Pease porridge in the pot,
Nine days old.
Some like it hot,
Some like it cold,
Some like it in the pot,
Nine days old.

Little Jack Horner
Sat in the corner,
Eating a Christmas pie.
He stuck in his thumb,
And pulled out a plum,
And said, "What a good boy am I."

Higgledy, piggledy, my black hen,
She lays eggs for gentlemen;
Gentlemen come every day
To see what my black hen does lay.

Simple Simon met a pieman
Going to the Fair.
Said Simple Simon to the pieman,
    "Let me taste your ware."
Said the pieman to Simple Simon,
    "Show me first your penny."
Said Simple Simon to the pieman,
    "Indeed, I haven't any."

Three wise men of Gotham
Went to sea in a bowl;
If the bowl had been stronger
This rhyme would be longer.

Wee Willie Winkie runs through the town,
Upstairs and downstairs in his nightgown,
Rapping at the window, crying through the lock,
Are the children all in bed, now it's eight-o-clock?

Jack Sprat
Could eat no fat,
His wife could eat no lean.
And so, between the two of them,
They licked the platter clean.

Peter, Peter, pumpkin-eater
Had a wife and couldn't keep her.
He put her in a pumpkin shell
And there he kept her very well.

Little Miss Muffet sat on a tuffet,
Eating her curds and whey.
Along came a spider, who sat down beside her,
And frightened Miss Muffet away.

Dickory, dickory, dare,
The pig flew up in the air.
The man in brown
Soon brought him down,
Dickory, dickory, dare.

There was an old woman
Lived under a hill;
And if she's not gone,
She lives there still.

Here am I,
Little Jumping Joan;
When nobody's with me
I'm all alone.

Little Tommy Tittlemouse
Lived in a little house;
He caught fishes
In other men's ditches.

Old Mother Hubbard went to the cupboard,
To give her poor dog a bone;
But when she got there, the cupboard was bare
And so the poor dog had none.

Little Bo Peep has lost her sheep
And can't tell where to find them.
Leave them alone, and they'll come home,
Wagging their tails behind them.

Pat-a-cake, pat-a-cake, baker's man,
Bake me a cake, as fast as you can.
Pat it and prick it and mark it with B,
And put it in the oven for baby and me.

Jerry Hall, he was so small,
A rat could eat him, hat and all.

Diddle diddle dumpling, my son John
Went to bed with his breeches on,
One stocking off, and one stocking on;
Diddle diddle dumpling, my son John.

Doctor Foster went to Glo'ster
In a shower of rain.
He stepped in a puddle,
Up to his middle,
And never went there again.

GLOSTER

All the king's horses
And all the king's men
Couldn't put Humpty together again.

Goosey, goosey gander,
Whither dost thou wander?
Upstairs and downstairs
And in my lady's chamber.

Hickory, dickory, dock!
The mouse ran up the clock.
The clock struck one
And down he ran,
Hickory, dickory, dock!

Jack be nimble,
Jack be quick,
Jack jump over
The candlestick.

To market, to market,
To buy a fat pig,
Home again, home again,
Jiggety jig.
To market, to market,
To buy a fat hog,
Home again, home again,
Jiggety jog.

Hey diddle, diddle!
The cat and the fiddle,
The cow jumped over the moon;
The little dog laughed to see such sport,
And the dish ran away with the spoon.

Georgy Porgy, pudding and pie,
Kissed the girls and made them cry.
When the boys came out to play,
Georgy Porgy ran away.

Jack and Jill went up the hill
To fetch a pail of water,
Jack fell down
And broke his crown,
And Jill came tumbling after.

Hush-a-bye baby, on the tree top.
When the wind blows the cradle will rock;
When the bough breaks, the cradle will fall;
Down will come baby, cradle and all.

Ride a cock-horse
To Banbury Cross,
To see a fine lady
Upon a white horse;
Rings on her fingers,
Bells on her toes,
She shall have music
Wherever she goes.

Old Mother Goose,
When she wanted to wander,
Would ride through the air
On a very fine gander.

There was an old woman
Who lived in a shoe.
She had so many children
She didn't know what to do.
She gave them some broth
Without any bread,
And spanked them all soundly
And sent them to bed.

Little Boy Blue
Come blow your horn,
The sheep's in the meadow,
The cow's in the corn.
Where is the little boy
Who looks for the sheep?
Under the haystack,
Fast asleep.

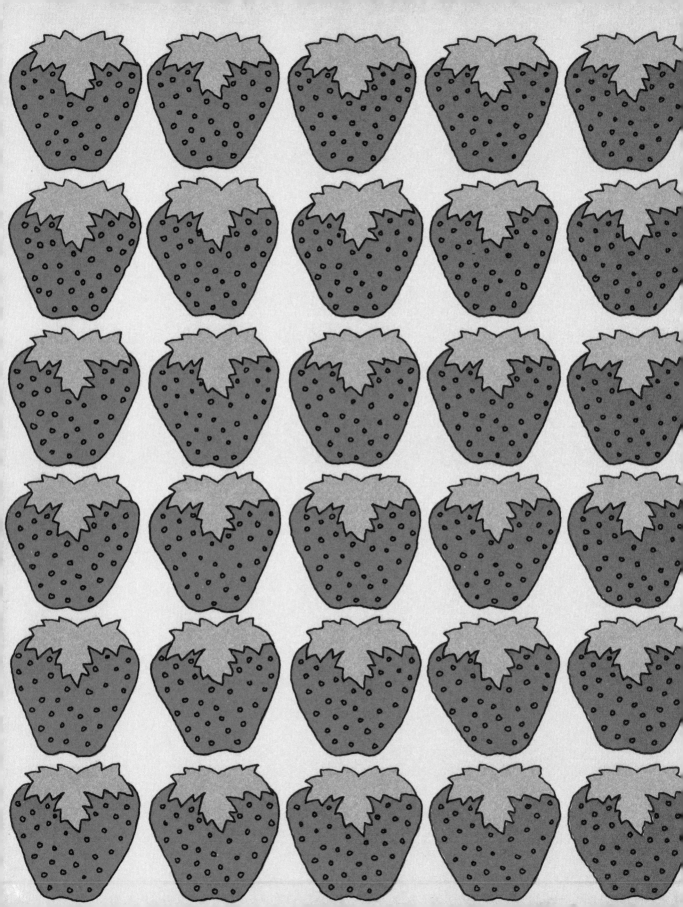